KU-545-842

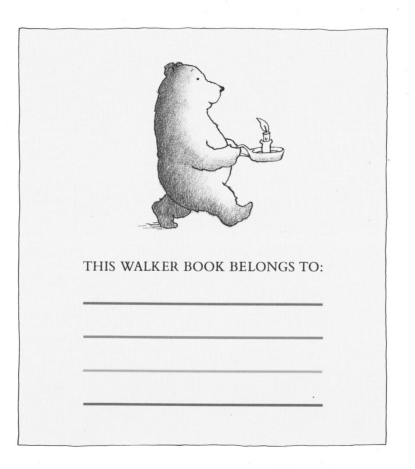

THIS WALKER BOOK BELONGS TO:

_____

_____

_____

_____

For Seth and Aphra

B.M.

For Mara, Liz, Amelia and David

H.C.

First published 1987 by Walker Books Ltd
87 Vauxhall Walk, London SE11 5HJ

This edition published 1989

Text © 1987 Blake Morrison
Illustrations © 1987 Helen Craig

Printed in Italy by Lito di Roberto Terrazzi

British Library Cataloguing in Publication Data
Morrison, Blake
The yellow house.
I. Title II. Craig, Helen
823'.914 [J]   PZ7
ISBN 0-7445-1361-8

THE
YELLOW HOUSE

WRITTEN BY BLAKE MORRISON

ILLUSTRATED BY HELEN CRAIG

WALKER BOOKS
LONDON

Every day we passed the yellow house
on our way to the park, Mum and
me and my little sister Jenny.
The house was on its own. It looked
old, sad and rather scary.

At the little wooden gate Mum would
lift me up to show me the garden.
There was a lawn, a goldfish pond,
a greenhouse, an apple tree, a dustbin,
a garden gnome. But never any people,
never any children.

One day Jenny dropped her teddy near the yellow house and Mum went back to fetch it. I climbed the wooden gate all by myself. Inside the garden was a boy in dungarees and a bobble hat. He waved to me.

"Come inside!" he shouted.
"Come and play with me."

I pulled myself over and slid my legs
down till they touched the pebbly path.
The garden looked huge. The boy stood
on the lawn.

"Come and see this!" he shouted.
"Come and see this."

I ran and looked. In the long grass
a tiger was playing with its cubs.
They cuffed and scratched each other.
They growled at me.

But the boy had moved off to the
goldfish pond.

"Come and see this!" he shouted.

"Come and see this."

I ran and looked. A white dolphin swam out from the lily pads, leapt in the air and splashed down on the water. It wiggled its tail at me.

But the boy had gone inside the greenhouse.

"Come and see this!" he shouted.

"Come and see this."

I ran and looked. A green snake was winding its body round the cane of a tomato plant. It shimmied and hissed. It stuck out its tongue at me.

But the boy was standing under the apple tree.

"Come and see this!" he shouted.

"Come and see this."

I ran and looked. A pelican was roosting
on a branch. It swallowed an apple with a
chomp chomp. It wobbled its pouch at me.

But the boy had opened the dustbin.
   "Come and see this!" he shouted.
      "Come and see this."

I ran and looked. Inside the dustbin
a panda was reading a newspaper.
It squinted and ho-hoed. It lifted its
hat when it saw me.

But the boy was striding through the
front door of the house.

"Come and see this!" he shouted.

"Come and see this."

I ran to look but the boy had closed the door. I stretched and stretched, right up on my tiptoes, but the handle was too high for me. I rang the bell but no one came to answer.

Now Mum had seen me and was calling
from the wooden gate. She looked cross.
I walked very slowly down the pebbly
path. Mum lifted me back over the gate.

"Where have you been?" she asked.
"Jenny was worried." Then Mum gave
me a great big kiss.

We still go past the yellow house on our way to the park, Mum and me and my little sister Jenny. Mum lifts me up to see the garden. There is a lawn, a goldfish pond, a greenhouse, an apple tree, a dustbin, a garden gnome. Never any people though, never any children, never the boy who waved to me. But I know one day he'll be there again calling me in to play.